Red, White, and Blue Jeans

The ★ 70s

A BARBIE DIARY OF THE DECADE

A GOLDEN BOOK • NEW YORK

Published in the United States by Golden Books, an imprint of Random House Children's Books, a division of Random House, Inc., New York, and simultaneously in Canada by Random House of Canada Limited, Toronto.

Library of Congress Cataloging-in-Publication Data
Lowery, Linda.
Red, white, and Blue Jeans / by Linda Lowery ;
illustrated by Ann Field.
  p. cm. — "A Golden book."
SUMMARY: In 1976, Barbie records in her diary the preparations she, her sisters, and their entire town are making to celebrate America's 200th birthday, including a disco dance, a parade, and a play, as well as other Bicentennial events they witness. Includes directions for making an apple-head doll and facts about life in 1976.
ISBN 0-375-82540-1
1. American Revolution Bicentennial, 1776–1976—Juvenile fiction. [1. American Revolution Bicentennial, 1776–1976—Fiction. 2. Fourth of July—Fiction. 3. Nineteen seventies—Fiction. 4. Diaries—Fiction.] I. Field, Ann, ill. II. Title.
PZ7.K25115Re 2005   [Fic]—dc22   2004015222
www.goldenbooks.com
PRINTED IN CHINA   10 9 8 7 6 5 4 3 2 1

Red, White, and Blue Jeans

The 70s

By Linda Lowery
Illustrated by Ann Field

 A GOLDEN BOOK • NEW YORK

May 21, 1976

Dear Diary,

America's 200th birthday is coming up this summer. It's our bicentennial—two centuries of independence for our country. Our town is throwing a humongous Fourth of July bash, and I love being part of it all!

We've done a lot of planning already, but now it's only six weeks away. We're down to the nitty-gritty. Big meeting tomorrow!

May 22, 1976

The town meeting was in the auditorium at my sister Stacie's school today. Everyone was there—little kids, teachers, parents, my friends, neighbors, and lots of veteran soldiers of World War II.

Since July 4 is on a Sunday this year, we voted to make the whole weekend a celebration. We set up a big blackboard. Then we wrote down plans for each day. Everybody called out ideas. Here's what we ended up with:

Friday, July 2: Disco Dance
Place: School gym
Theme: Stars 'n' Sparkles
Music: Disco
Decorations:

* Red, white, and blue streamers and balloons
* Huge cardboard birthday candles
* Silver stars
* Disco ball hanging from the ceiling

Saturday, July 3: Parade

Place: Main Street

Ideas:

- School bands, cheerleaders, and baton twirlers
- Fire trucks and floats
- A live Statue of Liberty
- Kids dressed in folk costumes from the countries of their ancestors
- Horses, clowns, and jugglers
- Veterans in uniform, carrying flags
- A birthday-cake float

Sunday, July 4: Fourth of July Fair
Place: Lakefront Park
Music: Dixieland band
Ideas:

- A play about the founding of our nation
- Demonstrations of Colonial American activities: doll making, rug hooking, butter churning, pottery making, and blacksmithing
- Picnics

Games with prizes:

- Three-legged race, pie-eating contest, etc.
- Fireworks over the lake

Doesn't it sound like fun, Diary?
There's my friend Christie at the
door. I'll write more later.

Still May 22, 1976

I'm back again, Diary. Christie came to talk about the Fourth of July parade. She's working with the war veterans. She also volunteered to be the Statue of Liberty on one of the floats.

Our neighbor Mr. Dibble can sure be a grump sometimes! I was surprised he even came to the meeting, since he usually stays at home. We were all very excited as we left the school. But Mr. Dibble was still grumbling.

"Too much work," he complained

to Mrs. Fox, the librarian. "Yes, I'm
an excellent whittler. And I have three
apple trees. But I can't be bothered
about making the clothes, too."

What? Clothes and apple trees?
I had no idea what he was talking
about. I wonder if he'll end up
helping.

May 23, 1976

Yesterday, everyone volunteered
to be on different teams. My sister
Skipper said she'd be the leader of
the decorating team for the dance.
I know she'll be great at it!

I volunteered to design the costumes
for the play. This is the perfect job
for me, since I love clothes and I love
sewing. Plus, my friend Kira is a
costume curator at the Philadelphia
Museum of Art. I'm planning to visit
her soon to get costume ideas.

Ken agreed to set up a blacksmith

shop exhibit. His great-grandfather
was a blacksmith, and his family
still has some tools he can use for
the display.

My little sister Stacie and her
friends formed an arts and crafts
team. They decided to make a
Bicentennial quilt. But just now Stacie
told me she has a really big problem.
None of the girls on her team can
sew! And they promised to make a
whole quilt for the celebration.
Something tells me I haven't heard
the last of this!

May 25, 1976

Earlier today, I was sketching some costume designs for the play when Stacie came and sat down next to me. I knew she wanted something. She was fidgeting with her pet rock, Rocky.

Pet rocks are a new fad. They are regular rocks, but they come in a box with instructions. Stacie and her friends take care of them as if they are pets. And for good luck, they talk or sing to them, and tuck them under their pillows at night. Crazy, huh?

Anyhow, Stacie started begging me to teach her how to sew.

"I'm going to be super busy designing and making costumes for the play," I told her. "But maybe I can squeeze in a sewing lesson or two for your team."

"Cool!" said Stacie. "We really need it. Thanks."

I think it'll be fun giving the girls some sewing tips.

May 28, 1976

I've decided to surprise my little sister with some big news. I'm taking her to see the Liberty Bell! Since I'm driving to Philadelphia to visit Kira, I thought it'd be fun if Stacie joined me.

We can leave as soon as her school lets out for summer. Also, I can help her on the trip with ideas for the quilt. I think she's going to be very happy about this.

May 29, 1976

I told Stacie the news. She was so happy, a grin spread across her face that matched her yellow smiley-face button!

"I need help with something else," she told me then.

Stacie said she had volunteered to write a patriotic poem. She's going to recite it in front of the whole town to introduce the quilt. I told her I'd be happy to help her, but first she'd need to go to the library this afternoon. She can get ideas for the

poem there and also check out some books on sewing and quilting. By the time we were done talking, she was heading for the door, on her way to the library.

June 5, 1976

It's almost time for our big trip.
Yesterday was Stacie's last day of
school. Summer has begun!

Stacie checked out a bunch of
books about quilting. We've studied
them every night. I suggested that her
team create a quilt that has a different
picture in each square. That way each
of the team members can make a
special square that will be part of the
finished quilt. Stacie thought that was
a great idea.

Well, I'd better get packing. . . .

June 6, 1976

We're bringing our sleeping bags in case we want to camp out on our trip. And we're bringing journals for writing and drawing. Stacie has already begun to jot down lines for her poem.

She's also bringing along fabric scraps and quilt squares to practice her sewing. She plans to draw ideas for the quilt every day. She's going to sketch whatever she sees along the way.

June 7, 1976

We were on the road by 6 a.m.—
I love getting an early start. It's
afternoon already, and we're at a
picnic table, having a snack. Stacie
is drawing the hot-air balloon we
saw today.

"What do you think?" Stacie just
asked me, holding up her picture.

"Right on!" I told her. A while
back we had stopped along the
roadside to buy cherry cider and fresh
honey. Nearby, a huge red, white, and
blue hot-air balloon was lifting off.

We've seen everything from farms with fruit and vegetable stands to cities full of traffic and skyscrapers. And we've counted license plates from almost every state—some of them were special Bicentennial versions, too.

Stacie and I talked about how weird it is to think that way back in 1776, none of this was here. It was all wilderness. There were Native Americans, prairies and forests, and wildflowers and animals. And now there are lots of different people, cars, roads, and farm stands.

Well, we have to get back on the road. . . .

Today we heard a staticky voice on our CB radio. We brought it just in case we ran into an emergency on the road. It's brand-new, and we're still learning how to use it.

"She's parked at the station in Jonesberg, good buddy," someone said on the CB.

We listened in as other drivers started talking on their CBs. They were talking about the Freedom Train. I explained to Stacie that the Freedom Train is a railroad museum

that's traveling across the country for the Bicentennial. It has lots of historical artifacts and exhibits. We realized that we were near Jonesberg, so we pulled off at the next exit. Sure enough, a silver train painted with red, white, and blue stripes was parked at the railroad station. Lots of people were waiting to go inside.

"What luck!" I said. "Let's stop here and check it out."

"Boss!" said Stacie. It's her favorite new word. It means "cool." She made a quick note in her journal and put it away. Then she tucked Rocky into her pocket, and off we went.

"All aboard!" the tour guide hollered. We stepped onto a moving walkway that took us through the train cars. George Washington's copy of the Constitution, Jesse Owens' Olympic track medals, President Kennedy's rocking chair, and Martin Luther King Jr.'s Bible were on display. We then walked through Ben Franklin's print shop and Thomas Edison's laboratory. We even saw a moon rock.

My favorite part of the museum was Abraham Lincoln's tall stovepipe hat. Stacie loved Dorothy's gingham dress from *The Wizard of Oz.*

June 9, 1976

Dear Diary,

We are finally in Philadelphia! There are lots of old buildings and brick streets. In some places, it feels just like we stepped back in time to 1776.

This morning, we headed to the Philadelphia Museum of Art, where Kira works. She told us that they had filmed a movie here about a boxer named Rocky who gets a chance to fight the heavyweight champion. Stacie thought it was boss that the boxer has the same name as her pet rock.

Kira's office is great. Since she is the costume curator, she has drawings and photos of old-fashioned clothes everywhere: on the desk, on the bulletin board, and framed on the walls. The clothing and accessories are all early American. Part of Kira's job is to make sure they stay in perfect condition. She repairs the clothes and keeps a catalog with a photo of every item.

Kira also gives tours, which she says is one of her favorite parts of her job. She took us to see the Three Centuries of American Art exhibit. Room after room was packed with

paintings, furniture, and clothes from the early days of America.

Stacie especially loved the dresses that looked like the ones they wear on *Little House on the Prairie*. That's her favorite TV show.

Kira said the prairie dresses were popular when pioneers began heading west in covered wagons. The dresses were plain and easy to take care of on rugged journeys. Before that, dresses were fancier.

Soon we came to the 1776 fashions. I drew women's fashions on one page of my sketchbook: low-necked dresses, petticoats, straw hats, and felt bonnets.

I drew men's clothes on another page: wool breeches, vests, long shirts with lace cuffs, and silver shoe buckles.

"These are clothes that were worn by wealthy people," Kira explained. "Now I'll show you simpler clothes worn by plantation slaves and other colonists."

There's so much to see, and so much to sketch. Gotta go!

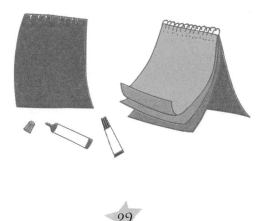

June 10, 1976

I'm back, Diary. The rest of our day yesterday was great. Kira invited us to take a museum tour with the DAR—the Daughters of the American Revolution. They're women whose ancestors fought for our country's independence. Stacie went with them while I stayed behind to work on my sketches.

I could hear the women of the DAR chatting as Stacie was introduced to them in the hallway. They were thrilled to hear about her quilt project.

They told her they'd answer any questions she had about the revolution.

I could hear my little sister. Why weren't there any founding mothers, only founding fathers? Couldn't someone figure out how to fix that crack in the Liberty Bell? Questions, questions!

One of the women answered that there were founding mothers. They just didn't sign the Declaration of Independence or draw up the Constitution. They were working to support the soldiers behind the scenes.

Well, my stomach is grumbling. It's time to have lunch. I'm hungry enough to have a Philly cheesesteak sandwich and then an ice cream sundae. Yum!

June 13, 1976

Stacie and I are getting ready to leave Philadelphia. We've had so much fun! During the last couple of days we've visited all the historic sites we could.

First we saw Independence Hall. That's where the founding fathers gathered on the afternoon of July 4, 1776, to sign the Declaration of Independence.

Next we headed for the Liberty Bell. Stacie told me that the Liberty Bell cracked the very first time it was rung. It was remade twice, but they

finally gave up trying to fix it. Stacie learned that from the women of the DAR.

Well, our journals are jam-packed with ideas. We saw famous buildings, cobblestone streets, and little brick row houses with gardens. All nice images for Stacie's quilt.

Of course, we also made time to go shopping. We found modern prairie dresses that are long and gathered. They look like the dresses on display at the museum. We think they're cool, so we each bought one.

Now I'm really excited about getting home and working on the

costumes. And Stacie can't wait to
start the quilt. I told her that tonight
we'll practice stitches. That's the way
a quilt would have been made in
1776—all by hand.

"People didn't use sewing machines
until after the mid-eighteen-hundreds,"
I told her.

"I know," said Stacie.

"Where did you learn that?" I
asked.

"From the women of the DAR,"
we said together, laughing.

June 15, 1976

On the trip home, we saw horses pulling covered wagons on the highway! One wagon had OHIO painted on it.

"Is that a real wagon train?" Stacie asked. Her eyes were huge. She couldn't believe what she was seeing.

"It's the Wagon Train Pilgrimage," I told her. I knew this was another spectacular Bicentennial event. The wagon caravan was heading to Valley Forge to meet other wagons to celebrate the Fourth of July.

We pulled off at the next turn
and found a huge field with covered
wagons parked everywhere. Just like
the pictures in our history books,
they had tall canvas tops and were
drawn by horses. They came from
every state in the union. We even saw
one from Hawaii.

A man and his wife came out to
welcome us. He was dressed in a
buckskin costume. She was wearing
a long cotton dress and a big blue
bonnet. They invited us to camp with
their group and have hot dogs, beans,
and biscuits for dinner.

"And I made apple cobbler for

dessert," the woman added, winking.

I didn't have to ask Stacie twice. She'd already pulled out her journal. She was sketching a big wooden wagon wheel.

All around us, people were busy tending to pioneer chores. Some hauled water from a pump. Others chopped wood for the evening campfires. Stacie and I helped feed the horses. Stacie's favorite horse was a cream and white pony named Buttermilk. "No, you can't bring Buttermilk home," I teased when Stacie gave me a pouty look.

"Bummer!" she said.

The sun is setting now, all orange and pink. Beautiful!

Well, I've got to go get ready for a pioneer evening by the campfire. I'll write more later.

P.S. to Diary: The pioneer man and woman showed us the Rededication Scroll, a special Bicentennial paper. It stated that we would uphold the values of freedom and democracy our country is based on. Lots of visitors had signed it. We sat by the fire and signed it, too.

June 16, 1976

We're home, Diary! Before I unpack,
I want to tell you about our pioneer
night. When it got dark, we set up
our sleeping bags to camp under the
stars. We put on our new prairie
dresses and sat by the campfire to
keep warm. At suppertime, we pulled
out the cherry cider and honey we
had bought at the beginning of our
trip.

"Honey for the biscuits!" I
announced. "Come and get it!"

Everybody shared what they had,

and we all felt like we were one big family. After supper, people began to sing and dance just like early American settlers. We joined in and sang "O, Susannah!"

Later, in the glow of the fire, we looked out at the covered wagons beneath the moonlit sky. I showed my sister how to stitch one of her designs onto a quilt square. We felt like pioneers. I know we'll never forget this special "sisters" time together.

The trip was wonderful. But my bed sure is comfy, and it's good to be home!

June 17, 1976

I can't believe how busy our town has been getting ready for the Bicentennial. The decorating team painted the fire hydrants red, white, and blue. They hung flags on every streetlamp downtown. And they strung red, white, and blue lights in the trees down by the lake. Everything looks beautiful!

I promise to write more tomorrow.

June 18, 1976

Everywhere in town, things are hopping! In barns and garages, teams are building floats for the parade. Stacie's team is quilting in one of the classrooms at school. I gave them a few basic sewing lessons, but the girls are pretty much on their own now. I am swamped with the costumes I have to make for the play.

People are busy in the school auditorium, too. That's where play rehearsals are being held. The play, of course, will be at the Lakefront Park

on the Fourth. It covers the history
of the United States, from Native
American life to the arrival of the
Mayflower pilgrims to the signing
of the Declaration of Independence.

Skipper's group is planning to turn
the gym into a magical place for Stars
'n' Sparkles night. They bought white
streamers, midnight blue balloons,
and shiny silver stars.

Ken and Alan helped out by hanging
a huge disco ball from the ceiling.
When the lights shine on it, sparkles
shoot all over the walls and floor.

My team set up tables with sewing
machines in a far corner of the gym.

We've been measuring and cutting
and stitching and trying on costumes
over our jeans. Busy, busy, busy!

Christie is going to portray Betsy
Ross, who sewed the first American
flag. Her costume has a white ruffled
bonnet and a blouse with puffy
sleeves. She found her calico skirt at
a garage sale. It's way too big, so I
tucked the waistband in at the seams
and pinned it nice and snug. Then
I worked on turning up the hem.

Now I'm on a little break. It's my
turn to play dress-up! I'm wearing
a pale blue printed prairie dress. I
feel like I should be back with the

wagons, sitting in front of the
campfire.

Time to work on more costumes. . . .

June 19, 1976

I just woke up, and I'm lying here in bed, thinking about how much fun I had yesterday. As I was working on Christie's dress, a sudden boom, like thunder, blasted off the walls of the gym. Skipper was testing the record player, and she was playing disco music.

"You should be daaan . . . cing, yeah!" the speakers blared. A group called the Bee Gees was singing. Skipper moved to the music as she organized everything for the dance.

Christie started dancing, too. I told her to stand still or her hem would be uneven, but she couldn't resist.

All around us, teams were dancing on the gym floor. As soon as the last pin was in, I jumped to my feet and Christie and I joined them.

"Hey, Betsy!" the guy playing George Washington called to Christie. "Let's dance!"

Pretty soon, Betsy Ross was twirling across the floor with George Washington. Ben Franklin was bumping shoulders with Pocahontas. Paul Revere struck a pose, his index finger pointing in the air.

Then another song blasted from the record player. Skipper danced over to me, singing, "Do the hustle!"

"Doesn't everyone look cool like this?" I shouted over the music. "It's a great mixture of old and new. At the dance, why don't you have some people wear clothes from 1776 and some from 1976?"

Skipper thought it was a great idea. Can't you just see the dance floor? There will be people wearing feather boas and buckled shoes, platform shoes and coonskin caps, white powdered wigs and pink glitter bangs.

Anyway, I decided I had better

hustle out of there and get going. I hung my costume on the clothes rack.

"Let's dance the night away!" I heard everybody singing as I headed out the door. It looked like my team was planning to do just that.

Reminder to myself

Pick up more fabric, beads, two wigs, buttons, and a feather pen.

June 21, 1976—8:00 p.m.

What a bummer day!

After buying all my supplies, I decided to check on Stacie and her team. When I walked into the room where they were working, it looked like the world was coming to an end.

The girls were all sitting around the table with sad faces. They were ripping stitches out with little scissors. The fabric stars looked like a dog had chewed on the edges. And the stripes were all crooked.

Whitney held up a quilt square. It

had something in the middle that looked like a little brown and white animal. I had no idea what it was, and I didn't want to hurt her feelings by asking. But then she told me it was supposed to be a covered wagon!

"Everything is horrible," cried Stacie. "Even my poem is crummy!"

Just then, Janet let out a gasp. Her mood ring had turned black. The other girls checked their rings and they were all black, too.

"What does that mean?" I asked. I know the girls love their new mood rings as much as they love their pet rocks. The stones in the rings change

color depending on how you're feeling. If the stone is green, it means you feel fine. Dark blue means you are very happy. I had a feeling I already knew what black meant.

"It means we're miserable!" said Whitney.

"Our quilt is a total flop!" wailed Janet.

"What are we going to do?" Stacie moaned.

I wished I could just sit down and fix all their problems. But I had bags full of fabric and buttons and costume pieces. And I had a to-do list a mile long. There was no way I

could be on two teams at once. I told the girls that they needed to take a break and think things through. But Stacie was afraid that if they didn't keep working, the quilt would never get done.

I told them nobody said they had to handle everything by themselves. They have a whole town full of people to count on. But the girls are absolutely certain that no one will want to help.

"Who's going to volunteer to be part of the biggest disaster of the whole Bicentennial?" Whitney moaned.

I told them all to go home and sleep on it. When they left, their mood rings were dark as mud.

You know what? Stacie just went to bed but her light is still on. I'm going to peek in on her. Be right back. . . .

When I said good night to Stacie, she was just taking off her mood ring. She stuck it in her pet rock box on the table next to her bed. Looking at her ring was just reminding her of how miserable she was feeling.

"Sweet dreams," I told her.

"Maybe I'll dream about my poem," she said. "What if it doesn't exactly rhyme?"

"That's okay," I said. "Not all poems rhyme. It just has to say what you want to say."

"But I have no idea what I want to say," Stacie said.

"You will," I promised her. "Now get some sleep."

Stacie picked up Rocky and gently petted the top of his . . . well, his little head. She stashed him under her pillow for good luck and rolled over to go to sleep.

I'm going to try to get some sleep, too. Nighty-night.

June 22, 1976

This morning I woke up with a great idea! I shot out of bed and knocked on Stacie's bedroom door. I told her I was going to give Mrs. Kimball a call. She lives right down the street—and I had just remembered that she's president of our local DAR.

"Right on!" called Stacie, jumping out of bed.

It turns out that Mrs. Kimball knows how to quilt and she had been hoping to be part of the celebration. She just didn't know if she was needed.

I told her she had no idea how much we needed her and how thankful we'd be for her help.

After I hung up the phone, I told Stacie the good news: "She'd like you and your team to meet at her house tomorrow."

"Boss!" said Stacie.

Stacie and her team are going to spend the whole afternoon at Mrs. Kimball's house. They'll bring everything with them, including the quilt squares, sketches, needles, and thread.

June 23, 1976

Today Mrs. Kimball surprised Stacie and her team by inviting some DAR friends over to help them.

When Stacie got home, she told me that they had all formed a quilting bee. They sat around the dining room table and stitched like worker bees. Mrs. Kimball and her friends also told the girls stories about the early days in America.

Stacie says Mrs. Kimball is eighty-three years old and used to make her own butter in a churn! She even

milked the cows in the morning. Then she used the cream to make the butter. I bet she baked her own bread for that butter, too.

Stacie also got to see a U.S. flag from 1818 that only had twenty stars on it. It belonged to Mrs. Tibbs's great-great-grandmother. It's amazing that there weren't any states established west of the Mississippi River at that time.

June 28, 1976

Things seem to be coming along very well with Stacie's quilt. Every day she comes home with little pieces of history to share. But she won't say anything more about the quilt. Tucked away carefully at Mrs. Kimball's, it's now a secret that nobody is allowed to see. Stacie says it's going to be a big surprise.

She doesn't know I have a surprise of my own for her. I've been sewing a flowered prairie dress and bonnet for her to wear when she recites her

poem. They are exactly like the ones she loved in Kira's museum. I can't wait to give them to her.

July 2, 1976—1:00 p.m.

Can you believe it? It's two days before the Fourth of July! My closet is full of freshly ironed costumes. Stacie spent all day rewriting the last lines of her poem. And Skipper's been hustling in and out of the house with stuff for the disco dance.

This morning, Skipper's arms were full of glittery paper flames for the birthday candle decorations. In the afternoon, her arms were piled high with bright feather boas for door prizes.

I can't wait for the dance tonight. I'm wearing my disco outfit. It's a shimmery white satin pantsuit with a matching vest. I'll also wear my tallest platform shoes. Ken will be going 1776 style—he's dressing like Thomas Jefferson!

Still July 2, 1976—Midnight

I'm back, and the dance was a smashing success! Skipper's team did a fantastic job!

When we entered the gym, we walked through a curtain of shiny silver beads. Inside, everything sparkled. The birthday candle decorations glittered on the walls. The twinkly stars dangled from the ceiling. The disco ball spun above the dance floor.

"This is just magical!" I told Skipper. "What a great party!"

"Thanks! Guess I'm just a disco queen!" she said, flipping her red boa over her shoulder.

Lots of people dressed in clothes from 1776. They danced with people like me who were dressed in 1976 disco clothes. Everyone had the best time! We all talked and laughed and boogied and hustled. And Skipper's door prizes went over great.

I'm so tired from all the fun that I can barely keep my eyes open. And this is only the start of the big weekend!

July 3, 1976

This morning, I was up at eight o'clock for the parade. The giant papier-mâché heads of Presidents Washington and Lincoln went first. Then all the war veterans marched and waved their flags. Following them were kids on decorated bikes, including my littlest sister, Kelly. There was a fife and drum trio, and even a guy dressed like Uncle Sam on stilts.

Just as the high school band was marching by, Ken came rushing over

to me. Christie had twisted her ankle and couldn't stand up on the float! She was going to be fine, but the float needed a Statue of Liberty right away. Ken grabbed my hand and ten minutes later there I was, hurried onto the final float of the parade.

I posed elegantly. I held a huge torch in my right hand and a big book in my left. My gown was lovely; my crown was regal. And guess what? I was green! My face and arms were painted to match the real Statue of Liberty. Everyone loved it.

July 4, 1976—4:00 p.m.

The Bicentennial party is almost over.
I think every single person in town
came down to the lake for the fair.
There were a pie-eating contest, a
three-legged race, and a bake sale.
Red and blue striped tents were set
up for the colonial arts and crafts.

And I finally solved the Mr. Dibble
mystery. Remember how he was
grumbling about whittling and apple
trees back in May? And I had no idea
what he was talking about? Well, I
passed by one of the tents, and there

he was, demonstrating a craft. He was making old-fashioned dolls with crinkly faces carved out of apples.

His display showed all the stages of creating apple-head dolls. First he peeled the apples and dunked them in lemon juice. Then he put them on Popsicle sticks and carved their faces with his pocketknife.

Behind him, stuck in a big flowerpot, were lots of apple heads that had been drying for weeks. They're cute and wrinkly and have the sweetest smiles.

"Hello, Mr. D.," I said cheerfully.

"Now I'm having fun!" he told me

with a great big smile. "I haven't made apple-head dolls since I was a kid!"

Just then Mrs. Fox, the librarian, joined him. "Aren't his dolls wonderful?" she asked. "I'm making their clothes."

"What a team!" I said. "I'll be back after the play to buy one!" It was nice to see them having such a good time.

As I walked to the stage that had been set up for the play, I checked out more exhibits. Stacie's art teacher was forming clay into bowls on a potter's wheel. Christie's dad was

demonstrating chair caning. The mayor's wife was showing people how to dip candles. When I got to the blacksmith tent, I saw Ken's grandfather teaching Ken how to shoe a police horse.

Then it was curtain time! We performed our play without a hitch. Well, maybe a hitch or two. At one point, the wind blew the wig off a British soldier. I had to run after it. Then Martha Washington tripped over her long skirt. But other than that, it was terrific.

After the play, no one wanted to take off their costumes. When I left,

everyone was wandering around the park dressed like Native Americans and colonists, servants and noblemen.

There's Stacie. She just came home to dress for the big quilt presentation. I've got to go get her surprise out of the closet now. Hope she loves it!

Night of July 4, 1976

Dear Diary,

It's bedtime now, on our nation's 200th birthday. As I'm writing this, I can still hear firecrackers blasting. In the distance, people are shooting off even more fireworks.

At dusk, Stacie and Mrs. Kimball walked up the gazebo steps, followed by the rest of the quilting team.

"This talented group ranges in age from seven to ninety-seven!" announced the mayor. "And wait till you see the wonderful work they've

done! I'm proud to say their project will hang in our town library for years to come."

The girls and women unfolded the quilt, and we all gasped. The disaster had turned into the best part of the whole weekend!

The quilt had twenty-four hand-stitched squares with images of America from 1776 and 1976. There are square patches showing the Alamo, the Liberty Bell, and the St. Louis Arch. There are a soaring eagle and a Native American peace pipe. There are a buffalo and a baseball glove. There are a supersonic

jet and a locomotive with steam
pouring from its engine. One square
is the hot-air balloon from my trip
with Stacie.

When the crowd was done *oooh*ing
and *ahhh*ing, Stacie stepped forward.
She looked terrific in the prairie dress
I'd made for her.

Stacie took a deep breath and recited her poem:

Our Freedom Quilt

by Stacie Roberts

A little bit of each of us
Is woven in this quilt.
We made it stitch by stitch—
The way America was built.
Mrs. Kimball's handkerchief
Turned into Plymouth Rock.
The sail atop the Mayflower
Was cut from Janet's sock.

Scraps of soldiers' uniforms
Became our battle scenes.
The purple mountains used to be
A pocket in my jeans.
We worked together side by side,
Stitching square by square.
We're proud to share our
Freedom Quilt
With people everywhere!

Everyone clapped and cheered
when Stacie was done. The girls and
the women of the DAR all held hands
and bowed to the audience.

Then it was time for the fireworks.
We all looked up and watched as the
colorful bursts filled the sky. I felt so
proud of my sister, and so proud of
my country—and especially proud of
my town.

Happy birthday, America!

How to Make an
Apple-Head Doll

What You Need

I large apple

I cup of lemon juice

I Popsicle stick or pencil

A kitchen knife

2 whole cloves or little beads for eyes

Directions

★ With an adult's help, peel the skin off
your apple.

★ Soak the apple in lemon juice for
   10 minutes.

★ Take your apple out of the lemon juice.
   Pat it dry.

★ Stick the Popsicle stick or pencil into
   the core. This will be used as a handle.

★ Using the knife, have an adult help you
   carve a face on the apple. Scoop out two
   hollows for eyes. Make sure to leave a hunk
   of apple in the middle for a nose. Cut a slit
   underneath the nose for the mouth.

- Press the cloves or beads into the hollows for eyes.
- To dry your apple, put the handle into a pot of sand or soil so that it stands upright. Leave it there to dry for 2 to 4 weeks. Every day it will shrink a little more. Soon a wrinkly face will appear.
- When the apple is dry, glue on hair that's made out of yarn or cotton.
- You can make the outline of the body with wire hangers. Or you can use a small plastic bottle filled with sand for a more solid body.

- Make clothes for the apple-head doll the way you would for any doll. Or just use clothes from another doll.
- Attach the apple head to the body by sticking the head on top of the wire body or the neck of a small plastic bottle.

Notes

- Your apple will shrink to half its size once it dries, so use a big apple and carve large features.
- You can make hands out of apple chunks, too—just use an extra apple.

★ If you live in a humid area, it is better to partially dry your apple head in the oven first. Leave the apple in a 200° oven with the door slightly open for 4 to 5 hours. Then let it air-dry for several days.

★ The apple will stay a bit soft, even when it's completely dry.

COOL
1976
FACTS

Gerald R. Ford

What was American life like in 1976?

★ Gerald R. Ford was our 37th president.

★ A loaf of bread cost $.35, a gallon of milk cost $1.65, and a first-class postage stamp was $.13.

★ The minimum wage for workers was $2.30 per hour.

★ **New stuff:** VCRs, computers, and home video games.

What did people care about?

Patriotism! The spirit of 1776 was thriving in 1976. Americans dressed up towns and cities in red, white, and blue for the nation's 200th birthday. Schools taught special American history courses. Families visited early American museum collections and saw shows about historical events.

Who was well known?

Jimmy Carter

With a winning smile and soft-spoken manner, Carter was voted into the White House as our 38th president. He defeated Gerald Ford in the November 1976 presidential election. Jimmy Carter had strong beliefs about humanity and ecology. He was named Man of the Year by *Time* magazine.

Olympic Athletes

Some of the athletes in the 1976 Olympics became very famous.

Nadia Comaneci: Teenage Romanian gymnast who was the first ever to score a perfect 10. Actually, she received seven perfect 10s! She won gold medals in the uneven bars, the beam, and the all-around competition.

Bruce Jenner: Called the World's Greatest Athlete after winning the gold medal in the decathlon.

Sugar Ray Leonard: Light welterweight boxing gold medalist.

Michael and Leon Spinks: Brothers who won middleweight and light heavyweight boxing gold medals, respectively.

Dorothy Hamill: Dynamic ice-skater whose short "wedge" hairstyle became a major fad. She won the gold medal in women's figure skating.

What was the big event?

The American Bicentennial! The year
1976 marked America's two centuries
of freedom from the British government.
The biggest bash of the year was
America's 200th birthday on July 4. It
overshadowed everything else that year.
A few once-in-a-lifetime national events
took place:

The American Freedom Train
crisscrossed the nation. It had a steam
engine and twenty-six cars. It carried
more than five hundred artifacts unique

to American culture. More than seven million people climbed aboard the train on its journey. Another forty million watched it roll along its route.

The Wagon Train Pilgrimage to Pennsylvania was a pioneer-style traveling event. Authentic covered wagons from each state crossed America. They followed the historic wagon trails that were blazed by westbound settlers in the 1800s. Musicians and performers put on shows at camps in towns along the way. Visitors could join in and contribute their talents. They could also sign parchment Rededication Scrolls, which proclaimed their commitment to America's principles of freedom.

Operation Sail in New York City's harbor was a grand parade of tall sailing ships from around the world. Six million people gathered on July 4 to view the awesome armada.

What was happening in the world of science?

Home Computers

Steve Jobs and Steve Wozniak designed the Apple I, and the first home computer was born. It was sold as a kit. It had no keyboard, case, or monitor. You had to put the whole thing together yourself.

The Apple II was based on the Apple I design and was built in 1977. The Apple II could display color graphics. It also had more expandable RAM and a beige plastic case.

Apple II

From 1976 to 2003 British Airways operated the Concorde on international flights.

The SST (Supersonic Transport)

The Concorde jet aircraft began passenger flights from London and Paris to Washington, D.C. It was now possible to fly across the Atlantic Ocean in less than four hours instead of eight hours. Traveling west through five time zones, passengers would arrive before they had taken off!

Mars Landing

On July 20, America's Viking I robot spacecraft made a first-ever landing on Mars. Scientists announced that the spacecraft had found signs of life on Mars. One photograph that was beamed back to Earth looked like a giant shadowy human face on the surface of the planet.

It was really just a mountain.

What kinds of music were people listening to?

Disco

A new wave of music called disco was becoming popular. Songs had a steady rhythm and a driving beat—perfect for dancing. The word disco comes from the French word *discothèque* (dis-ko-TEK), which means a place where records are collected.

Hit disco acts included Donna Summer and the Bee Gees. Some hit songs were "Disco Lady" by Johnny Taylor, "Turn the Beat Around" by Vicki Sue Robinson, and "That's the Way (I Like It)" by KC and the Sunshine Band.

Rock

The big rock star at the time was British guitarist Peter Frampton. His double album, *Frampton Comes Alive,* was number one for seventeen weeks.

Other Hits

The year's top Grammy Award winners were George Benson and Stevie Wonder. Top 40 hits included "Silly Love Songs" by Paul McCartney & Wings, "Don't Go Breaking My Heart" by Elton John & Kiki Dee, "Mamma Mia" by Abba, "I Write the Songs" by Barry Manilow, "Beth" by Kiss, and "Muskrat Love" by the Captain & Tennille.

What were some of the new dance crazes?

The hustle was a dance that combined flowing movements and quick turns and breaks. Partners danced the same coordinated steps, kicks, turns, and hand gestures.

The bump was also popular. Dancers moved up and down, and on the beat they would bump a part of their body together, such as their hips or elbows.

What were some of the fads?

Pet Rocks

If your parents didn't let you have a
puppy, you could buy a pet rock that
came with care instructions.

Mood Rings

The stone in a mood ring turned
different colors. Changes were triggered
by your skin temperature, which
changed with different emotions.

Smiley-Face Buttons

These buttons were bright yellow. They sometimes had the words "Have a Nice Day" printed on them, too.

CB Radios

America's new fad of chatting on CB (Citizens Band) radios while driving created new slang words. It also inspired songs like "Convoy" by C.W. McCall.

Time Capsules

To celebrate the Bicentennial, schools and communities buried containers to be opened in a future age. Inside they put pictures, papers, and items that represented life in 1976.

What were people wearing?

 Red, white, and blue clothes showed up in every store. Stars and stripes were popular on T-shirts, jeans, and buttons, and were even painted on people's faces.

Other Trends Were:

Disco Clothes: Guys wore polyester leisure suits, tight knit tops, and wide bell-bottom corduroys. Girls wore dresses or pants in shiny fabrics. Boas (named after the snake) were long, feathery scarves.

Granny Dresses and Prairie Skirts

Jewelry: Puka necklaces, made from bleached white seashells

Shoes: Platforms with very high heels

Hair: Teens copied the hairstyles of famous people. David Cassidy wore a long hairstyle on TV's *The Partridge Family*, and that's how a lot of guys wore their hair. Girls copied actress Farrah Fawcett's long hair and feathery layers. Some clipped their hair into a short wedge style like Dorothy Hamill's.

How were kids talking?

"Boss," "Neat," "Dy-no-mite!": Great!

"Bummer": A disappointment or Too Bad.

"Right on!": I agree!

"Humongous": Huger than huge

"Veg out": Relax

"Let's book": Let's get going.

"Boogie": To dance, disco style

"Ten-four, good buddy": In CB radio language, this means "I understand what you're saying, friend."

What new toys were kids playing with?

Action figures included the Bionic Man and the Bionic Woman, Muhammad Ali, and Stretch Armstrong. Hello Kitty became a trendy image, appearing on school supplies, backpacks, lunchboxes, dolls, and clothes. Atari's video arcade game called Pong was the first video game for home televisions.

What names were popular?

Top choices of names for boys were Michael, Christopher, Jason, David, and James. The popular girls' names were Jennifer, Amy, Heather, Kimberly, and Stephanie.

What books were kids reading?

Tuck Everlasting by Natalie Babbitt, *Dragonwings* by Laurence Yep, and *Pyramid* by David Macaulay. The

Caldecott Medal winner was *Why Mosquitoes Buzz in People's Ears* by Verna Aardema, illustrated by Leo and Diane Dillon. Adults were reading *Roots* by Alex Haley.

What movies did people go to see?

Some of the many big movies of the year were *King Kong* and *All the President's Men*. *Rocky* was filmed in just twenty-eight days and won the Oscar for Best Picture.

What were people watching on television?

Popular shows about pioneers and American families were *Little House on the Prairie* and *The Waltons*. Shows featuring strong women were *The Bionic Woman, Charlie's Angels,* and *Wonder Woman. Happy Days* and *Laverne & Shirley* were shows about the 1950s. And it was the first year for the popular program *The Muppet Show.*

Bicentennial Minutes were short patriotic vignettes shown every evening. Various celebrities would say, "Two hundred years ago today . . . and talk about historical events that led up to America's independence.

Bicentennial Trivia:
Did you know . . . ?

 There were originally fourteen American colonies founded by Great Britain in North America. When thirteen of those colonies declared their independence from the British crown in 1776, the fourteenth colony refused to join. What was the fourteenth colony?

Answer: Canada's Nova Scotia

Philadelphia, Pennsylvania, is where Betsy Ross sewed the first American flag. The Liberty Bell, a symbol of America's freedom, was hung in the tower of Independence Hall in the mid-1700s. It

cracked the first time it was rung. On July 8, 1776, the bell rang out to call citizens to the first public reading of the Declaration of Independence.

★ Some Native Americans in colonial America were tailors, gun stock makers, carpenters, and whalers. They worked side by side with pioneers. During the Revolutionary War, many Native Americans fought with the colonists. But most ended up with the British. Why? Answer: One reason is that King

George III tried to protect Native American lands from the colonial settlers as the settlers moved west.

★ The story of George Washington's having wooden teeth is not true. His dentures were fitted with ivory and real human teeth and held together with springs. They always caused him problems. His grim expression on the one-dollar bill doesn't mean he was cranky—he was just trying to keep his teeth in!

A BARBIE™ DIARY OF THE DECADE

Discover the Fashions and Fads of Barbie™

A blast from the past!